Grump and
That Mammoth Again!

Grump the Ice Age cave man is back, as cross as ever, in this latest collection of stories. Once again he goes through the trials of Ice Age living, made worse by the devotion bestowed on him by Herman, the great hairy mammoth. But Grump does have a knack of discovering new and wonderful inventions . . . especially when he is in desperate situations!

DEREK SAMPSON

Grump and
That Mammoth Again!

Illustrated by Simon Stern

MAMMOTH

Also by Derek Sampson

Grump and The Hairy Mammoth
Grump Strikes Back
Grump Goes Galumphing

First published in Great Britain 1981
by Methuen Children's Books Ltd
Magnet edition published 1986
Published 1989 by Mammoth
an imprint of Mandarin Paperbacks
Michelin House, 81 Fulham Road, London SW3 6RB

Mandarin is an imprint of the Octopus Publishing Group

Text copyright © 1981 Derek Sampson
Illustrations copyright © 1981 Simon Stern

ISBN 0 7497 0065 3

A CIP catalogue record for this title
is available from the British Library

Printed in Great Britain
by Cox & Wyman Ltd, Reading, Berkshire

Contents

I

Grump's Tootler

'Trunk off, trug nose! Why can't you ever
leave me in peace?'

Those words rang shrill and clear in the chill
air of an Ice Age day. They came from a small
caveman in a raggedy rabbitskin jacket.
Grump was his name and grumpy was his
nature. That wasn't his fault. Living in the far-
ago Ice Age made everyone testy. The cold
nibbled at their knees so, and chewed their ears
like a puppy with extra sharp teeth. No
wonder Grump was often bad-tempered.

He had other troubles, too. He was a very
odd-looking caveman, with a face like a
knobbly potato and a body like a broken
umbrella. The other cavemen never stopped
teasing him about the way he looked, and
long ago Grump had decided that nobody
liked him and he liked nobody. Today, for
instance, they had refused to take him
hunting.

'Take you along, bat ears?' they had

mocked. 'Not likely! A face like yours is sure to bring us bad luck!'

So they trudged off through the snow, leaving Grump cold and irritable and lonely as usual. That's when he found Herman standing behind him and that's when he had shouted his angry words.

'See what you've done! They won't take me because you'd be hanging round too!'

It wasn't true, of course, but Grump was seldom fair where Herman was concerned. Herman was so big and so easy to shout at. He was a mammoth, a sort of huge elephant badly in need of a haircut, and he was the friendliest creature who was ever born. What's more, everything Grump did fascinated him.

'You never leave me alone ... never!' Grump muttered. 'It's like being followed round by a great snuffling mountain.'

He gave a last goggle at Herman and marched into his cave to sulk. It was quite a comfortable cave as Ice Age caves went, with a fire in the centre to keep it pleasantly warm and fuggy, but right then Grump hated it. He sat on a stone by the entrance and glared out at the world. Across a clearing were the homes of the other cave people, with the women tidying and cleaning. By the lake children were playing and shouting in the sunlight. Farther on, the hunting party of cavemen was disappearing up the glacier. And there, his trunk swaying placidly, Herman was strolling into the forest. Grump's glare became angrier as he watched him.

'What I need is something to make old wrinkle-chops leave me alone forever, something that'll fry his fur with fright.'

He sighed as he remembered all of the tricks he had used against Herman – snowballing him, buffeting him, trapping him in a pit. None of them had worked, and somehow Grump had always ended in a worse mess than the mammoth.

'Not this time! I know exactly the thing to drive that dozy furbag away!'

Grump leaped forward with a squeal of delight as he spotted something in the jumble in a corner of his cave. It was a horn with a broken point from which he had once tried to make a cup. He shivered as he remembered the icy water dripping through the end onto his chest.

'But if I popped something in the big end and blew through the small end I reckon I could make it whizz straight at that mammoth.'

He slid a pebble into the horn and blew gently. The pebble flew out and clanged around the walls of the cave. Grump chirruped with delight. This was most satisfactory.

'Watch out, stone head,' he crooned, 'this is where I take the wrinkles out of your trunk.'

Grump giggled gleefully to himself and slipped from his cave to find Herman. For once it was not an easy task. It was almost evening before he came upon the mammoth in the forest not far from the caves. The sky was dark with grim clouds by then and snow was starting to fall, but that did not bother Grump. Nothing bothered him when he was up to mischief.

'I think I'll bombard him with snowballs,'

he decided. 'After all, I only want to chase him away, not hurt him.'

Still giggling to himself, Grump crouched behind a giant tree, scooping snow into handy horn-size lumps. Herman, meanwhile, meandered from tree to tree, his feet ploughing great ditches in the snow. He paused occasionally to drag down a tasty mouthful of leaves, and hummed to himself as he munched them. It was fun being a mammoth. Nobody was big enough to tell him that it was bad manners to eat and sing at the same time.

'He'll soon sing a different tune,' Grump sniggered. 'Grump the mammoth-mauler strikes again!'

He popped a snowball into the horn, pointed it carefully at Herman around the tree, and blew. Nothing happened. No snowball whizzed from the other end and sloshed the mammoth behind the ear. Grump blew again, harder this time. Again nothing happened. He frowned, filled his puny chest with air and blew with all of his strength. Something did happen that time. A snowball wobbled from the end of the horn and squidged feebly by Herman's feet.

Herman hardly noticed it. He was staring instead in amazement at the horn in Grump's hand. Grump was staring at it in amazement, too. Something else had come from the horn when he blew – a great mooing noise as if a cow had its tail caught in a gate. Grump put the horn nervously to his lips and blew hard again.

'*Wuuuooooo! Wuuuooooo! Wuuuooooo!*'

The sound hooted around the forest, startling birds into squawking scurries and making snow tumble from the trees. Herman shook his head, curled his trunk in delight, and tooted his trumpet call in return.

'Think you can out-tootle me, do you, tin-trunk?' Grump shouted in triumph. 'Not with my new noisemaker, you can't!'

His dire plans for Herman were completely forgotten. Now he skipped and danced from tree to tree, blowing his horn, making high notes, low notes, squeaky notes. And all the time the mammoth was tooting back happily. Heavy snow was falling about them and it was almost night, but they did not care. They had discovered a new game and they were happy.

Grump was just about to try a particularly hard howling note on his horn when he suddenly found that he was surrounded by white shaggy figures. He bounced backward in alarm.

'What? Eh? Snow ghosts! Don't hurt me, please!' he cried.

He paused, looked more closely, and with

relief recognized the other cavemen. They were weary and white with struggling through the snowstorm, and icicles hung from their craggy eyebrows.

'What's up, chaps? Didn't the hunting go too well?'

'It was awful, Grump, really awful,' one replied. 'We were completely lost in the storm until we heard that thing.'

Grump looked down at the horn in his hand in surprise, then played a specially fine note on it and smirked at them.

'You mean my tootle-horn? I've just invented it, for playing tunes and calling people home and things.'

'Then tootle us home right now, Grump,' the cave leader ordered. 'And in future when we're out hunting you stand by with your horn in case we get lost again.'

So that evening the women and children crowded from their caves to see a strange procession arrive. The hunters trudged wearily homewards bearing the food they had brought, and Grump marched at their head, proud as a bandmaster. His eyes were bulging and his cheeks almost exploding as he gave monstrous blasts on his tootle-horn. He looked very silly, but he didn't mind one bit – tonight he was someone important.

14

It didn't last, of course. He spoiled it all, being Grump. He played his horn all evening, long after the other cave people had gone to bed. The moonlit air was soon ringing with angry cries telling him to shut up and let sensible Ice Age folk get some sleep. He clumped his horn down by his bed and scowled.

'That's all the thanks I get for saving their lives,' he exclaimed. 'It's always the same. Nobody appreciates me!'

Someone did appreciate him. At that moment he heard a toot, just a faint toot, from outside his cave. Herman was there, saying how much he enjoyed Grump's new invention.

Grump grinned, gave one small answering toot on his horn, then snuggled down to warm sleep. Perhaps life was not so bad after all.

2

Grump's Cutter

'Fried icicles, I must be the cleverest caveman ever.'

Grump gave a little jig of satisfaction as he looked at the strange array of objects on a flat rock outside his cave. There was a stick with a specially sharpened end, an old deer's antler, a jaggedy rock or two, and even one of Grump's own teeth. He had broken that while chewing an Ice Age nut, and now it was fixed to the top of a stick and looked most peculiar. Grump rubbed his hands with glee.

'One of these should do the trick and give my poor old chumpers a rest.'

The idea had come to him while he was chewing a particularly tough piece of cooked coney rabbit. If only, he thought, he had something really sharp for slicing up his food. It would be useful, too, for cutting wood and scraping out tortoise shells and so on. That's when he had started his collection.

'Right, which shall I try first?' he pondered. 'Perhaps the pointed stick.'

He seized the stick eagerly and jabbed the sharp end across a piece of rabbitskin laid on the stone. The stick snapped. Grump frowned and peered closely at the rabbitskin. It was unmarked.

'Hmm,' he muttered, 'that didn't work. Not to worry, something will.'

Nothing did. Ten minutes later the rabbitskin was still intact and Grump was surrounded by scattered broken sticks, stones, antlers and old teeth. Grump was jigging again, but with fury this time.

'Blessed things, blooming rascally rats, none of them is any use!'

'What are you doing, Grump? You look even sillier than usual!'

Grump stopped his bouncing and whirled in alarm. He had been so angry that he hadn't noticed anyone approaching. Now he found himself squinting at the grinning face of one of the cave children.

'And what's your name, you cheeky prickle?' Grump demanded.

The boy grinned even more widely.

'Trug,' he said. 'Everyone here calls me Trug.'

'Well, Trug, why don't you go down to the

17

lake and play with the crocodiles?' Grump
suggested coldly.

Trug laughed and skipped twice around
Grump, quite unabashed.

'Crocodiles don't scare me,' he said. 'My
mother's name is Martha.'

Grump shuddered with dismay and gazed
uneasily about him. Martha was the biggest,
the fiercest, of all of the cave women. She
towered over Grump like an elephant over an

ant, and always looked as if she was thinking of stamping on him. He wanted nothing to do with her son!

'In that case, my ... er ... fine young lad, I'm going for a walk,' he declared, and hurried away.

It is a pity that in his agitation he did not look behind him. He would have seen Trug dogging his footsteps through the snow, dodging behind rocks or dancing around trees whenever the little caveman seemed about to glance back. Like Herman, Trug found Grump's continual antics fascinating.

Herman! Grump somehow knew he would see the mammoth sooner or later, and sure enough, there he was on the mountainside. He was strolling happily by the glacier, a great river of ice that creaked slowly downhill. As he did so he hummed like a mad bee, and here and there he plucked an icicle from the glacier's edge. Snap! The mammoth looked at the icicle in his trunk, then popped it into his large mouth. He strolled on again, rolling his cheeks appreciatively. Iced lollipops were just what a happy mammoth needed.

'What's that barmy buncruncher up to now?' Grump grunted, sidling forward for a closer look.

His eyes widened as he watched Herman.

'Of course,' he cried, 'just what I need for cutting with. Nothing is sharper than an icicle.'

That's why, when Herman reached up for another icicle he felt a strange sensation. Something seemed to be tugging fiercely at the fur on his mighty tree-trunk legs. He looked down mildly. Grump was clinging to his fur and pulling himself upwards like a crab trying to climb a ladder.

'Stand still, you lumpy larker! Just having a little climbing practice.'

Grump knew perfectly well that Herman would never allow that. Instead, the mammoth lowered his head to remove him gently, just as the cunning caveman had hoped.

'Got it!' Grump shouted with triumph and leaped from Herman, clutching the icicle which he had snatched from his trunk. 'Fooled again, bonebrain!'

He should have known better. Before he could dart away Herman's trunk swooped down and seized him. In a second Grump was dangling in the air, kicking, struggling, but still clinging to his precious icicle. Only the more he struggled, the hotter he became and the faster the icicle melted.

'Stop it, you hairy bully, you're ruining my cutter! Stop it or I'll ...'

Suddenly man and mammoth were stopped by a cry from nearby. It was a boy's voice, a very scared boy's voice, and it came from the glacier.

'Help! Please help me, Grump. I'm trapped.'

Herman squinted at Grump down the wrinkled length of his trunk, then whisked the caveman onto his broad back. Grump clung there as the mammoth scrambled onto the glacier and hurried towards the sound of Trug's voice. They peered together into a pit in the ice and saw the boy below them on a narrow ledge.

'Hallo, Grump. I fell down here and I can't get out.'

Grump chuckled. So much for the cheeky child who had mocked him! He didn't look so perky now. Well, let him stay there chilling his toes until someone came to rescue him, because Grump certainly wouldn't. He nudged Herman behind the ears with his knees.

'Come on, horsefeathers, get galumphing! I've got jobs to do.'

Herman did not move. His eyes looked down at Trug, then turned to stare at Grump reproachfully. Grump wriggled.

'Surely you don't expect me to help him after the rude things he said to me?'

Herman still did not move. The tip of his trunk whisked back and forth before Grump's face, and his eyes seemed to be pleading. Grump frowned guiltily until he could bear it no longer.

'Oh, all right then, but he doesn't deserve it. Lift me down and let's see what we can do.'

It wasn't too difficult. A minute later Grump was dangling into the pit from Herman's trunk and reaching down to Trug's uplifted hands. Soon the mammoth hoisted them carefully onto the glacier's edge.

'There!' Grump scowled, but truthfully he was feeling rather pleased with himself. 'Now get along home.'

It was a very subdued Trug who returned to the caves not long afterwards, and a very smug Grump who led him. By now he had quite forgotten Herman's part in the rescue, and was convinced he was a hero who had saved the lad from freezing. He smiled airily as Trug's mother emerged from her cave.

'Good morning, my good woman,' Grump announced. 'I've brought your dear little lad back to you.'

Trug's mother did not seem impressed. In fact she growled like an angry she-bear when she saw her wet and miserable son. Grump's

smile wavered as the furious cavewoman
stalked towards him.

'You don't understand, madam,' he
stuttered nervously. 'I'm a hero. I saved your
boy ...'

He didn't try to finish explaining. He turned
and darted into his cave, and Martha was just
behind him. He made it just in time, squeezing
through a narrow crack in the rocks into an
inner cave. Martha was too massive to follow
him through there.

She could attack him, though. Stones came whizzing through the crack at Grump, large flints which shattered and splintered around him. Grump danced and howled and dodged until Martha stopped her attack and grumbled back to her own cave. Even so, it was a long time before he dared emerge.

'There's gratitude for you,' he moaned. 'She almost pricked me to death with all those sharp flints.'

Sharp flints! Grump stared in sudden excitement at one of the shattered flints, and darted with it towards his cave door. The rabbitskin was still there on the flat rock, and Grump cut across it with the edge of the flint. The skin sliced gently into two. He had done it! He knew how to make something that was perfect for cutting!

'No more chumpering tough meat!' he cried. 'From now on I can cut anything.'

He was still crooning with delight when Herman saw him that evening. The mammoth wandered by the cave and was amazed to see the small caveman happily chopping up his supper – with a stone! Herman shook his head, and his tusks flashed for a moment in the firelight from Grump's cave. Then he trudged away in the moonlight to sit for a little and ponder a little on all that he had seen.

3

Grump's Bounce

'Cowardy cowardy caveman! Never been a brave man!'

The children were dancing in a giggling circle around Grump not far from his cave. He snorted indignantly. What a fuss just because he'd jumped when a snow goose had landed beside him. It hadn't been a very big jump. No cause for all this laughter. He drew his stubby body upright.

'Cheeky rompers! I'll have you know I'm not scared of anything.'

A boy grinned. 'Bet you are. Bet you wouldn't climb the moaning mountain.'

Grump turned pale. Nobody went near the moaning mountain, a huge volcano that thundered and smoked far away in the forest. Everyone knew that there was a fierce monster inside waiting to gobble up anyone who passed.

'I'd be happy to climb the silly old thing,'

he lied, 'but I'm busy right now collecting ...
er ... butterfly eggs.'

'Cowardy cowardy Grump! The snow
goose made him jump!'

They were at it again, dancing round and
round, up and down, until Grump's head
whirled and he could bear it no more.

'Stop!' he shouted. 'Just to prove I'm no
coward I'll climb the mountain this very
minute.'

They halted, suddenly scared at what they
had done. Grump was scared too, so scared
that his teeth almost jumped out of his head.
But he couldn't draw back now. He glared at
them darkly.

'I'm going, and when I'm eaten by the
monster maybe you'll be sorry.'

He wobbled away into the forest on trembly
legs. Soon the caves were far behind him, and
as he walked he grumbled his usual pitiful
complaint: 'Nobody likes me! Even the children want me turned into fried mincemeat.'

Grump was wrong. Someone did like him,
someone who was longing so much for him
to stop and maybe play a game or two. Herman had spotted Grump from afar while
munching an Ice Age apple. He hurried to meet
him. He had a new trick which he wanted to
show off.

It was a very good trick, really. By standing on one leg and blowing carefully Herman could keep a large nut floating just above the tip of his trunk. He was doing it when Grump walked into a clearing. It's a pity that Grump didn't actually see the trick, but his eyes were fixed glumly on the ground. He bumped into Herman, unbalancing him, and the nut fell smartly on Grump's head.

'That's all I need,' he wailed, staggering to his feet. 'A conjuring mammoth bombarding me! Out of my way, bone chops!'

He marched by Herman without another glance. The mammoth was very upset. His very best trick, and Grump had taken no notice. Perhaps the little caveman wasn't well? He hurried anxiously after Grump.

So midget and mammoth arrived at the foot of the volcano, and when he looked up at it Grump's knees did a dance of fright of their very own. The ground was so hot and it was rumbling and shaking. Peculiar plants grew with flowers as red as jellies. Giant bees busy-bodied from blossom to blossom. Birds darted like coloured lights between looping trees. Grump shuddered.

'This is all the children's fault! If I ever get back I'll never talk to those bullying bratlets again!'

Still, he had to go a little way up the mountain, just so that he wouldn't be ashamed. He clenched his chattering teeth and started climbing. Herman's eyes popped in alarm. Anyone knew that volcanoes were dangerous places to play. That nudge from the nut must have driven Grump senseless. He scrambled up the rugged slope in pursuit.

Ten minutes later, Grump seemed to be getting nowhere. No matter how hard he climbed, he always remained on the same spot. In fact he even seemed to be going backwards.

'Blessed place must be magic,' he panted. 'Feels as if something's pulling me downhill.'

Something indeed was pulling him. He looked over his shoulder. Herman's trunk was gripping his jacket and stretched more and more as man and mammoth pulled opposite ways. Grump wriggled and squiggled, but he was helpless.

'Let go, you crazy crane!' he cried. 'I don't need heaving anywhere.'

Herman would never have let go if Grump's scrabbling feet had not kicked up a cloud of dust. A little went in the end of his trunk and the mammoth sneezed with a mighty explosion. Grump flew through the air and skidded to a stop yards uphill. He bellowed back in triumph.

'Thanks for the lift. Like to sneeze me all the way to the top, would you?'

Herman had no intention of letting the small man reach the volcano's fiery top. He was sure by now that Grump had lost his wits. Dodging behind a rock, he lumbered out of sight up the slope. The higher he climbed, the hotter it grew, while the mountain grumbled and steamed menacingly. Suddenly Herman saw a large bush burst into flames and start to roll downhill towards Grump.

Grump, meanwhile, was feeling much braver and was actually humming. It wasn't such a bad old mountain after all. A bit noisy, maybe, and shaking, but as for that stupid story of a horrible monster . . . That's when he saw something awful rushing down at him! Herman had grabbed the burning bush and was now skidding downwards with it in his mouth. To Grump it looked like a fiery monster leaping at him through smoke and dust.

'The monster! The mountain monster is going to get me!'

His bravery was gone. His humming had stopped. He was fleeing down the mountain, not daring to look back at the terrifying creature behind him. He ran and ran until he saw a tree below him on the slope. Then he

leaped and landed high in its branches. The fiery monster whizzed by below and disappeared with a crash into the forest. All was silence.

Only then did he notice something odd. The tree was much too easy to cling to. In fact he could not let go. A sort of gummy stuff was oozing from the wood and holding him fast.

'What's happening? I'm all sticky and icky. Ugh, it's like swimming through porridge.'

And now the mountain was shaking again, violently. At least, the tree was swaying to and fro, up and down, so that soon Grump felt horribly seasick. He groaned and looked towards the ground. Herman was below, shaking the tree mightily.

'Stop it! Stop tugging around, you mouldy mattress! You'll have me off!'

That's exactly what Herman wanted. He'd saved the caveman from the burning bush. Now he had to get him away from this dangerous place. Gripping the tree firmly, he gave his biggest tug ever. It worked. Grump toppled from the branch.

But he didn't crash to the ground. The gummy stuff that had stuck him to the branch held him in a sort of cradle. It stretched slowly, longer and longer, until with a pop the strands broke. Grump had only a small way to fall.

'What a day!' he grumbled, picking himself up. 'A mad mammoth, a murdering monster, and now this horrid gum.'

He trudged downhill, muttering to himself as always and ignoring the relieved Herman. As he walked he plucked the rubbery sticky stuff from his jacket. Soon he had a large round lump of it.

'Good riddance!' he said, and flung it to the ground.

To his amazement it bounced into the air and jumped and bounded downhill like a mad kangaroo. He hesitated for a moment, his odd little face twisted in fascination, then ran after it.

There was a large band of children outside Grump's cave that evening to hear his adventures. The story was exciting, too, since he had made a few changes here and there.

'And what did you do when you met the fiery monster, Grump?' one of the children asked.

'Simple! I dumped it in the river and put its fire out,' said Grump, smiling loftily. Then he saw the children grin and nudge each other. Surely they didn't think he was telling lies? He reached into his jacket hastily.

'I brought back a new invention. I call it a ball. Quite fun, if you like that sort of thing.'

He tossed the lump of sticky stuff at a rock and it bounced away crazily. The children gazed after it, then dashed away with shouts of joy.

Grump settled back lazily on a warm rock. He was feeling most pleased with himself. Wasn't he the brainiest, bravest caveman ever? Only Herman, watching the cheering children throw the ball in the foggy evening air, knew any different.

4

Grump's Close Shave

'Turn me over, someone. I'm all toasted on this side.'

Grump moaned in delight and stretched lazily like a sleeping kitten. It had been a warm summer, far warmer than anyone could remember, and for once Grump was contented. His larder was full, his vegetable garden was flourishing, and his nose glowed pink with sunburn. He was a very happy caveman.

'Mmmm ... might even be nice to that furry old fathead if I see him,' Grump murmured sleepily.

He dozed for a few more moments, then sat up, his nose wrinkling in thought. Herman! Where was that nosy furbag? Usually he appeared at least once a day to make a nuisance of himself, but lately ... Grump scratched himself dozily and then crawled to his cave door.

The view outside was a very different one from usual. Because of the hot sun everything seemed to be melting. The snow on the mountain was turning into water that dodged downhill in a thousand rivulets. The lake had far overflowed its banks and flooded the clearing to the foot of every cave. The sound of running water was everywhere, as if every tap in the world had been turned on at the same time.

Grump frowned. 'And somewhere out there that gruff duffer is up to mischief.'

It was a worrying thought. Herman on the loose meant trouble for innocent cavemen sooner or later, Grump was sure. There was no escaping it. He would have to go out and discover what a certain mammoth was doing.

'Typical!' Grump grumbled. 'Thanks to old gruntle nut I shall get my toes all soggy.'

It would not be pleasant leaving his home. Because of the flood the Ice Age people had moved to caves much higher in the cliffs than before. Each cave had a ladder propped outside with its bottom standing in the water. And in that water were some strange animals. They had flat circular bodies and many legs, and they scuttled about like big angry spiders. They also enjoyed nipping cavemen's feet sharply, so that for days hardly anyone had dared leave the caves. Grump shuddered and stepped onto his ladder.

'Mind the crabs, Grump,' Trug bawled cheerfully from his own cave. 'They love playing nippy-toes.'

'I'm not scared, cheeky chops,' Grump called back airily. 'I've got my kicker-log.'

He climbed carefully down his wobbly homemade ladder to where a log floated on the water. He gave a quick suspicious look around. No nasty pinching creatures seemed to be about, so he sat astride his log and pushed away from the cliff.

'Look at me!' he shouted in triumph as he kicked his log along towards dry land. 'I don't have to stay indoors just because of some silly old crabs.'

The other people watched from their caves and were silent for once. They were certainly afraid of the crabs and they envied Grump his log boat. It is a pity that a busybody crab noticed his feet flashing in the water as the log neared dry land. Just to show he knew his job, the crab grabbed sharply.

'Oh! Oh, my favourite toe!'

Grump leaped ashore with a crab clinging sturdily to his big toe, then kicked and shouted until the animal was dislodged. He hopped around for a few more moments clutching his foot, then limped off with as much dignity as he could manage. The cave people chortled

and clapped cheerily. It was the first jolly thing they had seen in days.

'Nasty laughers! Mucky mockers!' Grump complained. 'And it's all because I had to come looking for that lumping mammoth.'

He was even angrier with Herman now. He'd certainly show that mammoth a thing or two when he found him! The trouble was, Herman was nowhere to be seen.

It was a strange Ice Age world that Grump searched that day. Because of the floods more and more animals crowded on to the dry land. Lumpy leathery creatures jostled against strange featherless birds. Lizards crouched in crevices, lazily blowing bubbles. Pterodactyls spread their steaming wings like great sheets to dry in the sun. And all had to dodge the crashing feet of dinosaurs who blundered around like fat grumpy aunts at a crowded party. Grump was soon almost exhausted.

'This sun ... never knew hot could be so horrible. It makes me feel all weak and sleepy.'

He was tottering with tiredness by the time he finally saw Herman. The mammoth was flopped like a giant rug in a shady pool. His eyes were closed, and his fur swayed like a bed of seaweed around him.

'Got you, lazy lugs,' Grump cried. 'Stop snoring and tell me what you're up to!'

By now he was too relieved at finding Herman to be angry with him. He even darted into the water and grabbed handfuls of the mammoth's fur to shake him.

'Wake up, you hairy whale, it's your

favourite caveman! Wake up or I'll tickle your tusks!'

Herman did not stir. Grump frowned, gripped more tightly and shook more violently. Still Herman's eyes remained closed. Grump's feet went cold in alarm. What had happened to the mammoth? Why did he lie there in a great soggy sleeping mass?

'It's the heat!' Grump wailed. 'It's made the silly beetler sick. He can't manage in that fur coat of his.'

Grump tried to imagine a world without Herman around to cause chaos, and he didn't like it. He had to do something to help the mammoth, to make him cooler ... like taking off his fur coat, for instance. Grump suddenly clapped his hands. 'Of course, my flint cutter! That should shave off his fur nicely.'

He wasted no time. His sharp flintstone was soon shaving Herman, and the world's first barber was at work. Large bare patches began to appear in the mammoth's fur, as if the giant rug was badly worn in many places.

It worked, though. Herman had been far too hot and would have been seriously ill without Grump's help. Now, as he cooled down, he recovered ... and he wasn't pleased.

'What's wrong, baldy? Why are you looking at me like that?' Grump cried in sudden alarm.

Herman had opened an eye, peered at a big bare spot on his shoulder, and was now glaring at the little caveman. It seemed to him that he had awakened from a pleasant sleep to find Grump stealing large lumps of his fur. There was only one way to deal with that!

'Wait, don't be hasty! I was only trying to help.'

Grump didn't waste any more breath trying to explain. Instead, he set off at a fine pace for home, with Herman hummocking behind him. He would never have escaped had Herman not still been sleepy. Even so, the mammoth was close behind Grump when he arrived at the flooded clearing. The nippy crabs were quite forgotten now. Grump darted through the water and sprang for his ladder.

He was near the top when Herman struck. The mammoth seized the ladder and shook it until it fell apart. Then he looked at his handiwork, trumpeted in seeming satisfaction, and sploshed away to rest somewhere cool again.

'What happened? I ... I'm split in two!'

Grump opened his eyes carefully. It was odd, but he still seemed to be in the air. The ladder was in two parts but he had not fallen. He had a long pole in each hand, and his feet rested on a rung that remained on each pole. He wobbled, but he could stand up high above

the water. In fact he found that he could actually walk about on the poles. He grinned and
yelled in excitement to the other cave people
watching from their doorways.

'See what I've done? I've invented these

things for walking high in the air. They're called ... stilts.'

Yes, stilts was the name for his wonderful new toy. Now he would be able to walk tall and peer into dodos' nests, to wade through water without getting wet, and to march through a whole army of crabs without getting pinched.

'Silly old nippers,' he cried, 'I'm safe up here and you can't get me!'

Not quite safe. At that moment Grump tumbled over backwards into the water. By the time he had scrambled back to his cave the crabs were nipping again – not at his toes, but at his bottom. Grump sat in his cave and rubbed himself ruefully.

'Even so, it was a good invention,' he told himself. 'Everyone's just jealous as usual.'

He settled down and tried to ignore the sound of laughter that came ringing from the other caves. He could bear it. He was used to laughter. Herman heard the laughter, too. He lifted his head sleepily for a moment, shook his ears, then settled back into his muddy pond for a long cooling doze.

5

Grump's Ghost

'Please, please don't eat me. I'm only a small caveman, and I wouldn't taste good!'

Grump was sitting up in bed, clutching his rough covers in fright and staring into the

darkness. A wind waved the flames of his fire and set shadows dancing on his walls. He shivered and peered towards a dim cranny. He was sure that he could hear something breathing there.

'Go away, please, mister ghostie,' he pleaded. 'You can have my best banger-drum if you leave me alone.'

There was nobody there, of course, but Grump had always been afraid of the dark. He went to bed each night convinced that a ghost would leap out and eat him. He awoke each morning certain that somehow he had escaped again. His fire only made things worse.

'It makes everything shadowy and scary. If only I had a good bright light so that I could see everything.'

Usually Herman was around at night, snuffling and being a nuisance, but lately at sunset he had headed off on his own business. Although he was sure that he really disliked his massive companion, Grump did miss him.

'At least with that gruff grunter about, no ghostie would bother me. He's got no right to go off and leave me!'

Grump hid his head for safety under his covers and grumbled in a muffled voice about Herman. He was still grumbling when he awoke next morning.

'Where does that woolly wanderer get to, that's what I'd like to know? He's ...'

Grump paused. Something was wrong. It felt like morning but it was very dim in his cave. He looked towards the door, then leaped up with a shout of annoyance. A large hairy body was completely blocking his door. Herman was leaning against the cliff outside and snoring with a sound like a jam-jar filled with bluebottles.

'Shove over, you dozy doorstopper! Move off or I'll make mammoth mincemeat of you!'

Grump pushed and shouted, bustled and bellowed, until finally Herman slowly opened his eyes. He bulged his head into the cave for a moment, looked reproachfully at Grump, and ruffled his hair with his trunk. Then he lumbered away to sleep in peace. He was a very tired mammoth.

'Serves you right for sneaking off all night and coming back covered in sticky stuff,' Grump called after him.

Sticky stuff! Grump stared at his hands. They were tacky with something from Herman's fur, something he had seen and eaten before. Honey! Now he knew where Herman went every night!

'The cunning tusker has found some honeybee nests and hopes I won't find them. Ho ho, honey tonight!' Grump yelled, dancing in delight. There was nothing he liked better than honey, and honey stolen from Herman was even sweeter.

So that night, when the mammoth set off for his secret honey hoard, someone was following. It was Grump, flitting from tree to tree just like the ghosts he always feared. Herman was uneasy. He sensed that someone was behind him but could not be sure. He tried tiptoeing into the shadows to wait, but a mammoth tiptoeing was about as quiet as a bear dancing on a dustbin. Grump easily hid until Herman started again.

Even so, Grump was not happy. No sensible person went out into the Ice Age night. There were too many animals roaming the dark looking for a crunchy snack. They were noisy, too, roaring and grumbling and sometimes howling impatiently. Grump wobbled with fright at every noise. After all, he could not be sure that it was just an animal.

'Maybe that ghostie's waiting to pounce,' he shivered. 'Must stay close to Herman.'

That was easier said than done. The closer Herman got to his honey, the more agitated he became and the faster he lumbered. Grump was soon having to run to stay close. At last he tripped over a creeper and skidded on his face until he banged to a stop with his nose against a rock. By the time he picked himself up, Herman had vanished.

'Where's that magical monster gone to now?' Grump wailed, rubbing his nose ruefully.

Grump's gaze searched the darkness in vain. He had almost decided that he had lost Herman forever when he suddenly heard a strange noise. Actually, it was two noises and he knew them both. One was the sullen buzz of angry bees, and the other was a maddening noise he heard almost every day of his life – the humming of a happy mammoth.

'He's out there somewhere!' Grump exclaimed. 'Watch out, honeypot snitcher, here I come!'

He darted forward into a small valley, his mouth dribbling at the thought of the dripping delicious honey awaiting him. All he had to do was find Herman, and ...

He stopped abruptly, for suddenly the night ahead of him was not dim any more. Something was lighting up the sky like daybreak. It was as huge as a house, and feathery, and glowed as if a million candles were burning all over its body. Worst of all, it was heading straight for Grump! He paused for a moment, his jaw trembling, then turned and fled with a yell.

'It's the ghostie! The mad muncher has got me at last! Someone save me, please!'

There was nobody to save him. Grump darted frantically about the forest, feeling as if he were running ten ways at once. And always the giant glowing ghost seemed to be just behind him, slow but purposeful. Only after a while did Grump notice that it was humming.

'Funny,' he muttered, slowing a little, 'ghosties don't hum. They sort of just grab and gobble you up.'

He snatched a peek over his shoulder, then came to a breathless halt. There was no ghost behind him; it was a happy mammoth, placidly trundling along and humming as it savoured a large honeycomb in its mouth. And why was Herman glowing? Thousands of fireflies had settled on his honey-sticky fur and were supping in the sweetness.

Grump shuddered in relief and let Herman snuffle by him. Still humming, the mammoth crunched into the night, shining like a giant walking bonfire.

'Now I've got to find where that great glowing jelly got his honey from,' Grump decided.

It was not difficult. Here and there Herman

had dropped dollops of honey, and fireflies still clung to them, marking a shining trail. Grump giggled as he hurried from one bright marker to another, heading into the valley again.

'Thought he'd fool me, did he? Ha ha, this way to honeyland!'

Then he found it, and suddenly he was not thinking of honey any more. In a clearing at the end of the valley stood a solitary tree. An angry cloud of bees still buzzed around it to show where Herman had called for his honey. But something far more wondrous than that was in that valley. The air was filled with shining fireflies, millions of them, dancing and swooping in the night. It was like having a sky filled with stars close enough to touch.

'It's beautiful,' Grump breathed. 'If only I could have a light like this in my cave at night!'

That's when he noticed a honeycomb on the ground. Hundreds of fireflies were clinging to it and glowing with satisfaction as they sucked at the honey. Grump swooped with a shout of triumph and snatched up the honeycomb, brandishing it in the air.

'I've got it!' he cried. 'I can have a light now whenever I want one. I'll never be afraid of the dark again!'

He ran through the forest joyfully, waving

the shining honeycomb above his head, and all around him it was as if a giant lamp had been switched on. He was not nervous now. Nothing could frighten him, no animal or silly imaginary ghost, while he had his light. He was still shouting cheerfully when he arrived back at his cave door.

It was blocked.

'Why, you mouldy mammoth, you're doing it again, except now I'm stuck on the outside. Move over!'

No use. No matter how much he pushed and cajoled, Grump could not rouse Herman. He did not try too hard. After all, the mammoth

deserved his sleep. He had helped Grump to make his wonderful new discovery.

At last Grump snuggled down in Herman's fur and went to sleep himself, and the fireflies danced over them until dawn came.

6

Grump's Thunder

'Bonk! Bonketty bonk bonk, bonk bonk!'
Grump stopped beating his log drum with a stick and looked upwards hopefully. Then he sighed and shook his head. Nothing had changed. Purple bruised clouds still crowded the sky, and thunder grumbled, but no rain fell. None had fallen for months.

'Bonk! Bonk bonk, bonketty bonk!' He banged again, but less hopefully this time. He just couldn't make rain. If only he knew how the thunder did it! Not that the thunder had done too well lately. No matter how much the sky rumbled no rain followed. That was why Grump had had the idea of helping with his drum.

'But I expect my drum's too weak to make a proper noise. But golly, if it doesn't rain soon we'll all be fried to crispy chips!'

Grump climbed to his feet with a groan. The unusually warm summer had long ago stopped being an exciting surprise. The lake by now

54

had shrunk to a few muddy pools, the snow had gone from all but the highest slopes, and Grump's garden was a drying desert.

'All I need is a little drop of water to make my plants prim and perky,' Grump moaned. 'But where's it to come from?'

He looked about him at the baked world bleakly, until suddenly a mischievous grin began to crinkle his lips.

'Of course, that big hairy watering-can! He's a four-legged rainstorm all by himself.'

Waving his hands in delight, Grump ran to the shrunken lake and plopped around in the porridgy mud until he had found what he was looking for. There was Herman, slumbering in one of the few remaining pools. Only his trunk waved, like an inquisitive worm, just above the water.

'About time that woolly wallower had some exercise,' Grump chuckled to himself. 'Now, how to do it?'

It was quite simple, really. Herman could not bear to have the delicate tip of his trunk tickled. It was delightful but painful, like having your toes chewed gently by a thousand friendly ants. Grump snapped a branch from a large fern onshore, leaned over the pool, and started slowly to tickle.

'*Splurgghh!*' Herman exploded from his

muddy bed like a rocket fired from a milk-
bottle. He scowled, gave a mighty shake that
darted mud everywhere, then glared around to
see who had disturbed his cool sleep.

'It was me, scratchy pants!' Grump shouted,
dancing nearby. 'Take your tusks to the
cleaners, you mangy mammoth!'

Grump knew what would happen. Herman
took one look at his capering tormentor,
sucked in a vast trunkful of water, and set off
in pursuit. For once Grump did not try to
escape too quickly. He darted instead, still
mocking and laughing, just out of Herman's
reach, until they arrived at his garden. Then

he turned, put his thumbs in his ears, and pulled his most horrid face.

'Tatty old carpet-bag! Your mother had moth and your father had falling hair!' he shouted gleefully.

At that he dodged aside, and it was as well that he did, for Herman fired a trunkful of water that would have had the little caveman spinning. It had worked just as Grump had planned.

'Fooled you, cottonhead,' he cried. 'You missed me and watered my garden instead. Look at it now!'

When he turned to look at his garden,

however, Grump was not quite so gleeful. Herman's water jet had torn some of the plants from the earth, and the rest lay, still dying, as the water steamed away from the hot ground.

'My garden! You've ruined my garden, you great clumsy waterblower!' Grump wailed.

Herman blinked. He had been disturbed from an innocent sleep, goaded into chasing a crazy caveman through the sweltering afternoon, and now he was being shouted at. It was really too much! He reached forward, blasted a bellow into Grump's ear, then trudged off in search of somewhere cool.

Grump jumped at Herman's bellow, but not as much as usual, for he had noticed something strange. When Herman made that noise he was certain, almost certain, that a drop of rain had fallen. Grump looked up at the sky again.

'I was right. My drum really wasn't noisy enough to make it rain,' he breathed. 'I need a bigger, noisier, drum.'

He knew just where to find a really big, really thunderous, log drum – on the mountain overlooking the cliffs above his garden. He had once seen a huge hollow log there, high on the hill where the snow had still not melted. The bigger the log, the louder the bang, and the more he would help the thunder to make it rain. He smirked. These things were quite easy when one was a very clever caveman.

An hour later Grump was trudging up the mountainside above his garden. He had to be careful, for the snow all about was melting and dripping miserably, but soon he saw the log lying on the hillside. He peered in at the top of it, and crowed.

'A lovely log, just what I need. I'll just clear out those stones that are jammed inside ...'

Grump slid down inside the log and started happily to stamp the stones free. He had been busy for some time before he noticed that it had become dim inside the log. He looked upwards and gasped.

'You again, trucky trunk! What do you want with me this time?'

Herman meant no harm. He had been dozing in a bed of snow nearby when he spotted Grump at work. Naturally he was interested and went to look. It was not his fault that his gently nudging face in the top of the log started it sliding.

'What are you doing, you silly pusher?' Grump demanded. 'I don't want to go anywhere!'

It was useless for Grump to argue and protest. He was trapped in the log as it slid down the mountain faster and faster towards the edge of the cliff below. He closed his eyes. Any moment now it would reach the edge, fly off, and ...

The log did not fly off. At the very edge of the steep drop to his garden below it jammed between two rocks. The log stopped, but Grump went on. The bed of stones on which he was crouched inside the log flew from the end and he followed them. He would have tumbled far down, but he grabbed the very end of the log as he flew out. He hung there, muttering.

'My poor plants, my lovely garden. If I fall I'll make an awful mish-mash of it – and myself!'

There was worse to come. The log had scoured a deep channel where it had zoomed down the hillside. Melting snow soon started to dribble into that channel, first in a trickle, then in a stream, and finally in a torrent. And it all poured through the log into Grump's face!

'*Glulurgle!* Drowning! Never been so clean ...'

He could not hold on; finally he let go and fell. It was almost a pleasant feeling, really. His eyes were closed and he told himself that he was a leaf floating in the autumn wind, or a pterodactyl going for a pre-supper spin. He

might have enjoyed himself, but for the thought of hitting the ground.

Phlunk! Grump stopped falling with a jerk, and decided that hitting the ground was not so bad after all. Or had he landed in a tree? He seemed to be swaying. Grump opened one cautious eye and found himself looking at the two anxious eyes of a mammoth. Herman had slithered down the mountain just in time to catch the caveman in his trunk.

'You again!' Grump cried, struggling to the ground. 'I was almost mish-mashed because of you!'

Grump did not care that Herman had probably saved his life. He felt much too foolish at what had happened for that. Besides, something else was distracting him. The cave children had rushed to his garden and even now were capering under the water that poured from his log-pipe above. Trug jabbed his arm gleefully.

'A waterfall for us to cool under, Grump. This is your best idea yet!'

Grump gazed at the children dancing under the water tumbling onto his ruined garden. Why did his plans never work out as he intended? Oh, well, he would find a way to make it rain some other day. Meantime, the waterfall looked very inviting. Soon he was jostling there, and soon he saw Herman looking at them wistfully. Grump waved.

'Come on, lobbylugs!' he called. 'I forgive you. Room for one mammoth under my waterfall.'

They were all still playing there that evening when a final clap of thunder shook the air and rain started gently to fall. The long summer drought was over at last.

7

Grump's Whizzer

'Toot! Toot! Toot!
I'm a charming young chap in a rabbitskin
                                        suit.

Toot! Toot! Toot!
I may look like an owl but I don't give a hoot!'

Grump was crooning to himself and looking
contentedly at the world below him. He could
see a lot from his perch – the children splashing
in and out of a warm pool nearby; the women
gossiping and dusting every rock thoroughly
outside their caves; and their husbands, far off
across the lake, fishing through holes in the
ice. Grump could see all this because he was
seated high, dangerously high, in a tree, but
that did not worry him.

'Quite safe,' he told himself. 'Can't fall with
this tied around me.'

He tugged at a rubber rope tied around his
waist, with its other end tied to the tree. Then
he reached into his pocket for his tootle-horn

and placed it to his lips. It was time to get to work.

'*Tootletooletooooo!*'

At the blast of his horn every bird nested in the trees around him squawked into the air and zigzagged across the sky. Grump giggled, pocketed his horn, and rubbed his hands. Now egg-collecting could begin.

It had really been one of his better ideas. Food had been hard to come by lately. Winter had returned like an old enemy. Animals to hunt were scarce, and even coney rabbits kept well away from hungry cavemen. There were always eggs to be collected, but the best nests were in the highest branches of the tallest trees. No caveman could risk being pecked by a fierce Ice Age bird and tumbling a long way to the ground. No caveman but Grump, that is.

'I just scare the birds away with my tootle-horn and use my rubber rope to keep me safe. Clever fellow!'

Grump swung cheerfully from tree to tree, scooping eggs from the deserted nests. That was the beauty of his rubber rope. He had made it from the gummy stuff he had found on the moaning mountain, and it stretched as far as he wanted.

'Time to blow my horn to scare the birds

away,' Grump decided, looking around him. 'They hate my tootling.'

Grump was right, the birds disliked his tootling. What he forgot was that another animal loved it. Herman was far away, munching a branchful of mulberries, when he heard the first toot. He cocked his head for a moment, then set off at an eager trundle. He was soon among the trees.

'*Tootletooletooooo!*'

Herman gazed about him, very puzzled. He could hear Grump but could not see him. The noise seemed to come from somewhere on high in the branches, but as far as he knew the little caveman could not fly.

Then a startling thing happened. Grump suddenly appeared right in front of his eyes, paused for a second, then disappeared again

– upwards! Herman blinked. What was this amazing new trick Grump was playing? There he was again! Grump shot down from the branches, stopped some way above Herman's head, then flashed back out of sight. Herman twitched his ears. Was he imagining things? Perhaps he had eaten too many mulberries.

He was not imagining things. Grump had fallen from a branch until his rubber rope stretched to its limit, then bounced up again. A few more lessening bounces and he was able to climb back onto the branch breathlessly.

'That was fun,' Grump decided when he had recovered his breath. 'Must try it again.'

Grump was bored with collecting eggs by then. His rabbitskin jacket was already bulging with them. Besides, rubber rope bouncing was far more interesting. He moved to another branch and jumped off gaily.

Those next minutes were the strangest Herman had ever known. Grump seemed to be everywhere, bobbing up and down before his eyes like a mad yo-yo. Herman darted from spot to spot, always just too late to seize the bouncing caveman. It was quite by accident that on one bounce Grump's jacket caught on Herman's tusk. The mammoth grabbed with his trunk.

'Hey, what's happening?' Grump muttered.

68

'I should be going back up but I'm slowly going lower and lower.'

He looked behind him. Herman was there, his eyes popping with effort as he pulled Grump downwards.

'Hey, what are you doing, you tugging rug?' Grump bellowed. 'After my eggs, are you?'

The rubber rope was at its full stretch when Grump's wildly kicking feet touched the forest floor. Dust flew into Herman's trunk, he sneezed and released Grump's coat, and the little caveman started his journey upwards again, faster than ever before.

'Oh, I'm flying! I'm flying and I won't stop until I hit the moon!'

It was as well that Grump's rope snapped. He crashed upwards through the branches and into clear sky before the rubber parted. He seemed to hang in the air for a moment, then slowly started to spin downwards towards the pool where the children were playing.

They were very taken aback by his arrival. Suddenly a brown yelling figure pitched into the water between them. It bubbled under water for a moment, then staggered to its feet. They looked closely. It seemed to be Grump, but usually even Grump was not splattered from head to toe in egg-yolk.

'What's up, Grump?' Trug demanded cheerfully. 'Dropped in for some scrambled egg, have you?'

Grump said nothing. He glared at the children, glared at Herman, who had emerged anxiously from the trees, then squidged grimly homewards. A certain mammoth was going to pay for what had happened to Grump!

If Herman had a failing, it was his curiosity. That was what made it so easy for Grump to set a trap for him next day. Herman was strolling through the forest when it happened. He stopped suddenly. There before him was a small snowman, and it seemed to be poking out its tongue at him. Herman touched it with his trunk. Yes, it was definitely poking out its tongue, and there beyond it was another snowman, and another, and another. This definitely needed investigation. Herman lumbered forward.

'Got him!' giggled Grump. 'Here's where I make the world's woolliest omelette!'

The idea had come to him while he was flying through the air. If a rubber rope could whizz a man, it could whizz an egg even better! That morning he had picked out a small tree, slim and straight, with two branches dividing in a V shape from the top. He had tied some rubber rope at the top of those branches and had – a catapult! When he put an egg in the rubber, pulled it back and let go, it had flown simply miles!

'And now I'm going to give that lumpy loon all the eggs he wants – in his eye!'

He had an egg ready in his catapult and some more in a neat pile behind him. The second that Herman appeared he heaved back

71

the rubber and – the tree snapped and Grump fell backwards.

Herman did not hear a thing. He was far too busy wondering why someone had bothered to build a line of snowmen making rude faces. At last he decided that he would never know. He sighed and hummocked away, rather disappointed. Meanwhile, the person who had built the snowmen to lure him on was sitting down in a crushed pile of eggs.

'He's done it again,' Grump wailed. 'That tusky rascal has egged me all over!'

What's more, his catapult was ruined. It had snapped off just below the V-shaped branches. Grump marched from the forest, muttering and pulling the rubber from his ruined catapult. As he came into the open, he glared at the useless piece of wood in his hand.

'Wretched thing! That's the last time I invent anything. What's more, I'll have no supper again tonight!'

He hurled the piece of wood far from him and strode away, but he had taken only five steps before something hit his neck. He turned with a howl, expecting to see Herman, but there was no mammoth behind him. There was only the bent piece of wood he had thrown away.

'Funny, how did it get back here? It must be some kind of magic.'

He threw the stick again, watching it this time. It skittered just above the ground, turned slowly in a circle, then plopped in the snow near his feet. Grump bent forward excitedly to snatch it up.

'This is wonderful!' he exclaimed. 'I'll be able to hit things far away with this ... even coney rabbits!'

Grump was deliciously full after his supper of rabbit stew that evening, full enough to boast loudly to the other cave people of his splendid new invention, the boomerang. They took no notice. They were used to Grump.

Herman heard the noise, but he took no notice, either. He was snuggled in the snow pondering a mystery. Why had someone built that line of little snowmen, and why did each of them have its tongue poking out so cheekily? It was very, very puzzling ...

8

Grump's Carving

'Gumboils galore, that face is ugly enough to be Grump's!'

Grump scowled and turned sharply. He knew that voice only too well. The cave children were standing behind him and Trug was at their head. He was pointing to a pile of snow nearby, lying against a shallow cliff-face, and he was right. If you looked closely you could see a twisty nose, two monkey-eyes, and large ears that looked like Grump's. Grump was not flattered.

'Can't you find something to do?' he asked Trug coldly. 'Can't you help your mother chew a few rocks for tea?'

Grump was in a very bad mood that day. All of the cave people were in a bad mood. A herd of dinosaurs had taken to tramping through the clearing outside the caves each night, and everyone was short of sleep. Only Trug seemed as cheerful as ever. He grinned.

'Mother's busy, Grump,' he said. 'Practising

throwing things into the lake for the next time you annoy her.'

Grump winced. However grumpy he was he had no desire to annoy Trug's fierce mother. He would sooner play tag with a woolly rhinoceros. He forced a smile and patted Trug's head.

'Then run along and play with my log drum,' he said. 'Make as much noise as you want.'

It always worked. Of all Grump's inventions the children liked his drum best, because it was so delightfully noisy! In two seconds Grump was left alone with the pile of snow that looked like him. He regarded it thoughtfully.

'It is like me, but it's not handsome enough. That nose needs changing, for instance, and the ears ...'

Grump was at work straight away, carving with stick and stone to make the snow more lifelike. Naturally, he improved the snow-face a little to make it more charming, more handsome, more as he imagined himself to be. At last he was satisfied with his work.

'There,' he declared, 'the perfect picture of a good-looking caveman. Bet that would fool old hairy-horns!'

Something Grump had often noticed was

that if ever he was thinking of Herman, there the mammoth would be. This time it was the same. Grump felt warm breath on his cheek, a chin resting lightly on his shoulder, and saw a trunk flicking past his ear towards the snow-face. Herman gazed at Grump's carving, peered at his face, then looked at the carving again. Grump chuckled.

'Can't tell the difference can you, silly dust-bin? I'm a good carver, I am. Why, I could make a mammoth!'

He did it, too. In no time he had carved a huge figure from a nearby heap of snow. It had a trunk, a curly tail, tusks, and it gleamed as the snow turned slowly to ice. Herman circled the silent white mammoth in wonder as Grump leered in triumph.

'There's a new pal for you,' he announced. 'Maybe in future you'll play with it and leave me alone!'

Grump spoke more truly than he knew. Herman did not leave the mammoth statue all day. Even when the gloom of night fell he stood contentedly by it, his trunk swaying in a slow friendly way. Grump watched from his cave door.

'Silly noggle thinks it's a real mammoth,' he chortled. 'Well, let them both freeze out there!'

Yet as he snuggled down under his bed-covers he was uneasy. Somehow he could not forget that soon the dinosaurs would start their nightly march right past where a certain foolish mammoth was standing.

'So what do I care if they barge the woolly whacker to pieces?' Grump asked himself. 'He's nothing to me.'

Even so he found himself a little later slipping from his cave and running as quickly as his banana-curved legs could go to where Herman stood.

'Get moving, floppy lugs!' he bellowed.
'The mammoth-mashers will be here at any
moment!'

Grump was tugging at Herman's hair, heaving and pulling like an ant trying to topple an
oak tree. The mammoth took no notice. He
had found a new friend, and he was happy.

'But he's not real, you loon! Look, I can pull
his trunk off!'

That is just what Grump did, snapping the
trunk from his carved mammoth and waving
it before Herman's face. Herman snorted and

scraped the brittle snow with one blunt foot. His new friend was now a trunkless new friend, and nobody treated his friends that way. Grump was going to pay for this!

'Sorry I can't stop. Urgent appointment!' Grump cried, and scampered off.

It was not only fear of Herman that sent him on his way. In the distance was the rumble of a large army of dinosaurs. Their nightly march was about to begin!

Grump was breathless but pleased by the time he was back in his cave that night. He had escaped from Herman, and Herman had escaped from the trampling dinosaurs. What was more important, Grump had a good idea.

'If old trundle toes thinks my mammoth was real, maybe I could fool a load of dinosaurs. I'll try tomorrow.'

The cavemen stopped in amazement on their way to fish in the lake next morning. At the entrance to the clearing by the caves all of the children were gathering large mounds of snow. Grump was already patting and carving some of the mounds into icy hardness.

'Wasting time as usual, grunt ears?' one of the cavemen said. 'What's the barmy notion this time?'

Grump looked down at him haughtily from a pile of snow.

'You'll see, my good man,' he promised. 'I call it my mighty dinosaur stopper.'

The cavemen were even more amazed when they returned that evening. The entrance to the clearing was jammed with snow-statues of dinosaurs, great ones, small ones, fierce and angry ones. A whole horde of dinosaurs made of icy snow seemed to be charging away from the caves. Grump stood by, rubbing his hands proudly.

'Impressed?' he asked. 'The silly dinosaurs will meet this lot tonight and think they're real.'

The men shook their heads in wonder.

'But what if they do?' one demanded.

Grump smirked. 'Don't you see, all my dinosaur statues are pointing away from the caves? The real ones will think they're going in the wrong direction and turn back.'

Grump was right about one thing. When the dinosaurs arrived that night, they did mistake his statues for other dinosaurs. He was wrong about another thing. The real dinosaurs did not turn back. They attacked his statues with such a growling and gnashing, such a roaring and smashing, that nobody got any sleep at all.

Grump was not very popular in the morning.

'Beetle brain!' they called after him. 'Sleep

wrecker! Another trick like that and we'll boil your ears!'

Grump did not stay to see if they meant it. He hurried off, muttering unhappily. Why was it always like this? Why did nobody ever appreciate him? No wonder he was grumpy all of the time! He wandered along, sadly kicking the snow, until he saw a familiar figure.

'Are you still here, gloomy moon?' he sighed. 'Still pining for your trunkless chum?'

Herman looked at him sadly. He was standing close to the statue Grump had made, nuzzling it, puzzled that without its trunk it no longer looked like a mammoth. Grump shrugged.

'Well, if a trunk is all you need, I'll soon supply that. Move aside, flop chops!'

Five minutes later Herman was cheery again. He was leaning happily against the snow mammoth. It was a fine animal now, with a splendid new trunk that Grump had fashioned.

'You're easily satisfied,' Grump complained. 'You've got a snow-chum and you're happy. I've got nobody.'

Nobody except ... Grump paused for a moment, then hurried off, his odd little face crinkled in pleasure. There was someone, someone he had made himself. Five minutes

later he was seated before the first statue he
had carved, the statue of himself. He looked
again and sighed with pleasure.

He really was a most handsome caveman!

9

Grump's Dream

'Go away! Go away, all of you! I never want to see you again.'

Grump was waving his fist and shouting from the door of his cave. He had to stand on tiptoe to do it, because he had piled logs in his doorway so that nobody, not even Herman, could come in. He only wanted to be left alone.

'Nobody would come near me, anyway, except maybe Trug or Herman. Not that I care. I prefer to be alone.'

Grump kicked discontentedly at his drum and plonked down by his smoky fire. He had been having a particularly bad time lately. The cave people had been specially unkind to him, and even the children had been more mocking than usual. As for Herman, he had taken to following Grump so closely that the caveman felt that he was dragging a big boulder at his heels wherever he went.

'I bet he's out there right now!' Grump

squinted into the darkness outside his cave. 'He wants to curl his trunk over my fire.'

He looked back into his cave. Sometimes he felt it was the warmest, cosiest home in all the Ice Age world. But tonight it was just a cold dark hole, its damp mossy walls shadowed by the flickering fire.

'If only I lived far far from here, a long long time from now,' Grump sighed sadly. 'Oh, well . . .'

He climbed into bed, wriggled down on the dry leaves that served as his hard mattress, and slept. And as he slept, he was gradually not in his cave any more. Slowly he found himself in a world he had never known and would never see again. The strangest thing of all was that, as it was happening, Grump knew that he was in a dream, yet it was a dream so real that he would never forget it.

'Funny place,' he murmured in his sleep. 'What's . . . Grump . . . doing . . . here?'

He was walking along a wide smooth grey path between high cliffs. There were holes in the faces of those cliffs, lots of them, just like the cave doorways he knew so well, but somehow different. He looked more closely.

'They're covered with a sort of shiny stuff you can see through. Must be some kind of magic.'

He was staring at the shiny stuff when he heard the noise. It was a sort of growling and roaring like a dozen sabre-toothed tigers. Grump gawped in horror. Racing towards him was the worst monster he had ever seen. It had two huge eyes, great metal teeth in front, and instead of legs it had wheels on which it was rushing at him. It was going to eat him! Grump did not hesitate. He dodged into a narrow gap in the cliffs and ran and ran until the roaring was long gone. He stopped and panted in relief.

'Never seen anything like that before. Phew, that would crunch you to bits in no time!'

When his fear had died a little, Grump looked around him again, and nearly tumbled over in surprise. He had run into a different place now. The cliffs were lower and stood around a square. There were wheeled monsters, too, but silent ones, gathered in long orderly rows. Most amazing of all, there were people, real people, strolling about as if not one bit afraid that the monsters would eat them. And their clothes! They must have been made from the skins of the brightest coloured rabbits that had ever hopped in the world.

'I never knew there could be so many colours,' Grump gasped. 'It's like a thousand sunsets rolled into one.'

He was feeling easier in this curious new world by now. He even walked among the people, and though they looked at him with interest, nobody bothered him. As he walked Grump looked into some of the caves in the cliffs through the shiny hard stuff, the glass. And what he saw there made his poor Ice Age stomach ache with hunger.

There was food, great heaps of food such as Grump had never seen. There were trays of meat, and bread, and food in gaily coloured packets, and orange, golden and green piles of fruit. What's more, the people were going into the caves and being given food by smiling assistants waiting inside. Grump could hardly believe it.

'They don't have to hunt for their food here, it's just given to them!'

Grump was never one to waste a chance. If food was being given away, he would be first in the queue. He hurried inside one cave, giggling in delight, and grabbed four shiny apples. Then he looked around. What should he have next? Some meat, perhaps, and some of those deliciously smelling things that the people around him were calling cakes, and some of those crunchy red things in a jar, and ...

'Hoy, what are you doing, you scruffy scrounger? Put those things back!'

Grump looked up. The smiling man behind the food was not smiling any more. He was frowning and gesturing angrily at Grump.

'You pay for what you have here, friend, or I'll have the law on you. Hey, come back!'

Grump was running again, but not from monsters this time. He was running from the man, who was waving and chasing him, and other people were running and waving, too. In all of the times he had fled from Herman, Grump never knew a chase like this. The whole world seemed to be after him and shouting.

He dodged down alleyways, skipped around trees, and ran round and round until his head was spinning. Once – most terrifying of all – he found himself running across a place filled with wheeled monsters. They charged at him from all directions, and he was sure they would have eaten him if he had not been so quick.

'Must hide ... can't totter any farther,' Grump gasped.   He staggered at last through the giant doorway of a large building that stood by itself. There was a word written over the doorway, the word MUSEUM, but Grump did not know what that meant. He only knew that he was tired and needed to hide. He leaned against a wall, panting, hoping that at last he was safe. He had never felt so lost, so lonely. All he yearned for was to escape from this noisy dangerous world, to see once more the things that he knew so well. That's when he saw a familiar face staring at him from across the room.

"Herman!' he cried. 'Herman, you've been here all along, you lumpy trundler!'

It was not Herman. Grump was staring instead at a life-size painting of his old companion. It hung on the wall opposite him, and beneath it was printed:

MAMMOTH — AN EXTINCT PREHISTORIC
ANIMAL

Grump could not read, of course, but something inside told him that there were no Hermans, no lumbering gentle mammoths in this world in which he found himself. At the thought, there was a hollow pain in his stomach that nothing could fill. He moved towards the painting and touched its rough surface tenderly.

'Where are you, crinkle-chops?' he whispered. 'Where did you and your silly noddle-head go? Oh, Herman ...'

'Oh, Herman ...' Grump was still whispering those words when he awoke next morning. He sat up and looked about him cautiously. There was his log drum, there was his turtle-shell saucepan, there was his sputtering fire. He was home! Home from that horrible dream world, wherever it was!

'Hallo, everyone, isn't it a lovely day!'

The cave people looked up from their work, shrugged, and looked down again. It was only Grump, being odd as usual. Grump was not worried. He was too busy bounding to where the children were drawing rude faces with burnt sticks on a rock wall. He nudged Trug cheerfully in the ribs.

'Not bad, Trug, you young rogue,' he said. 'I'll show you how to do it properly later.'

Trug was startled, but Grump was already skipping away like a happy fawn. Trug grinned. Grump was a crazy little caveman, but he was fun.

Grump was indeed crazy. He was crazy with joy to find himself in his familiar world, with its wide clean spaces and white untouched snow. He was even crazy to see Herman. The mammoth was standing placidly by the lake, fascinated by all of the colours he could see reflected in the dark ice.

'Wake up, sleepy nut!' Grump shouted. 'Wake up and take some exercise. Chase me!'

He swung on Herman's trunk like a bell-rope, then darted away. Herman twitched his ears with interest. He could never understand Grump. One moment he was horrid, and the next he was laughing like this. Still, if Grump wanted a game, he was always willing.

So they ran together, man and mammoth, chasing each other in circles in the sunlight of the Ice Age world.

You can see more Grump books
on the following pages:

Grump and the Hairy Mammoth

Tough though he is, Grump finds life in the Stone Age a tricky and often surprising business. Dripping icicles, cold feet and uncooked food are all problems he has to contend with. Added to this is his running battle with Herman the hairy mammoth, and Herman, despite his size, is far from stupid!

The vigorous, knock-about humour of the stories and illustrations will delight all those who are ready for something a little out of the ordinary. Grump, more by luck than judgment, usually wins through, and Herman is as endearing as only a mammoth can be.

Illustrated by Simon Stern

Grump Strikes Back

Grump, the Ice Age caveman, finds life difficult in the ice and snow, and matters aren't improved by Herman the hairy mammoth. Ever on the lookout for some fun, Herman always seems to do the wrong thing, and Grump is always complaining. But Herman often helps Grump make the most important discoveries which, quite by accident, end all his adventures.

This is the second book about Grump and is as slapstick and original as the first, *Grump and the Hairy Mammoth*. Together with Simon Stern's witty drawings, the stories add a completely new dimension to our knowledge of the Ice Age!

Illustrated by Simon Stern

A Selected List of Titles Available from Mammoth

While every effort is made to keep prices low, it is sometimes necessary to increase prices at short notice. Mammoth Paperbacks reserves the right to show new retail prices on covers which may differ from those previously advertised in the text or elsewhere.

The prices shown below were correct at the time of going to press.

☐	416 96490 7	**Dilly the Dinosaur**	Tony Bradman	£1.99
☐	749 70166 8	**The Witch's Big Toe**	Ralph Wright	£1.75
☐	416 95910 5	**The Grannie Season**	Joan Phipson	£1.75
☐	416 58270 2	**Listen to this Story**	Grace Hallworth	£1.75
☐	416 10382 0	**The Knights of Hawthorn Crescent**	Jenny Koralek	£1.50
☐	416 13882 5	**It's Abigail Again**	Moira Miller	£1.99
☐	749 70218 4	**Lucy Jane at the Ballet**	Susan Hampshire	£1.50
☐	416 06432 9	**Alf Gorilla**	Michael Grater	£1.75
☐	416 10362 6	**Owl and Billy**	Martin Waddell	£1.50
☐	416 13122 0	**Hetty Pegler, Half-Witch**	Margaret Greaves	£1.75
☐	749 70137 4	**Flat Stanley**	Jeff Brown	£1.99
☐	416 00572 1	**Princess Polly to the Rescue**	Mary Lister	£1.50
☐	416 00552 7	**Non Stop Nonsense**	Margaret Mahy	£1.75
☐	416 10322 7	**Claudius Bald Eagle**	Sam McBratney	£1.75
☐	416 03212 5	**I Don't Want To!**	Bel Mooney	£1.99

All these books are available at your bookshop or newsagent, or can be ordered direct from the publisher. Just tick the titles you want and fill in the form below.

Mammoth Paperbacks, Cash Sales Department, PO Box 11, Falmouth, Cornwall TR10 9EN.

Please send cheque or postal order, no currency, for purchase price quoted and allow the following for postage and packing:

UK	55p for the first book, 22p for the second book and 14p for each additional book ordered to a maximum charge of £1.75.
BFPO and Eire	55p for the first book, 22p for the second book and 14p for each of the next seven books, thereafter 8p per book.
Overseas Customers	£1.00 for the first book plus 25p per copy for each additional book.

NAME (Block letters) ....

ADDRESS ....

....